Autumn Verses

Collection of poems

Deepali Mehndiratta

Delhi – 110089 (India)

First edition : 2019

ISBN : 978-81-941351-1-1

Publisher
Prakhar Goonj
H-3/2, Sector - 18
Rohini, Delhi - 110089.
Ph : 7838505899, 7982710571
Email id : prakhargoonj@gmail.com
           sinha.neelu123@gmail.com

Autumn Verses
By
Deepali Mehndiratta

Dedication

I would like to dedicate this book to my mother who has always stood by me like a pillar of strength and supported me in all my endeavours, to my son Shivank, for always showering me with his unconditional love and also to my friends who always appreciated my work and encouraged me to write.

AUTHOR'S PREFACE

We humans go through myriad emotions in our life. It is sometimes not necessary for us to go through all the emotions but we can still feel the pain others are going through. We can feel the turmoil they are experiencing. In order to understand others we need to be empathetic and put ourselves in their situation.

I have always felt the complexities of human emotions deeply. There are a few of us who feel everything a bit too much. We humans possess a lot of complex emotions. To understand others we need to delve into the intricacies of their soul. My poems depict these complex emotions experienced by us in our lives. They have an inherent sadness in them.

Deepali Mehndiratta

Index

WOMAN

On some days I am on top of the world
On some days I am the best I can be
On some days I barely survive
On some days I am just me
Let me live the way I want
Not how you want me to be...

LOVE YOURSELF

No one will come to wipe away your tears

No one is going to treat you the way you
want to be treated

No one is going to love you the way you
want

No one will understand you the way you
want to be understood

No one will ever understand your silence,
the language of your heart

So love yourself, understand yourself

Live for yourself

Alone we are and will always be

Be your own best friend.....

LOVE

A day of love

Why should there be just one?

Love makes the world go round

It is the reason we feel alive

The reason we smile

The reason for our very existence

Everyday should be a day for love

As love never dies

It is there with us till our last breath

In some form or the other

Let love not be bound to just one day

Let's celebrate love every single day

ONE DAY AT A TIME

One day at a time

That is how I am taking it

One day seems brighter

But the next day

Am broken to pieces

By the thought of you

Sometimes it seems I can go on

Sometimes I can't even breathe

I feel suffocated to the core

By your absence

One day I feel I have gotten over you

The next day your memories cling on to me

Tell me how I am supposed to live like
this

One day at a time....

WINTER

It's the time of the year

When everyone wants to be

Enveloped in the warm blanket of love

A touch, a caress, a warm hug

Goes a long way on a cold winter day

Winter is a time when everything around is
bleak

Except for the love and humanity

Which makes it better

A hot coffee and snuggling up with a loved
one makes it worthwhile

Blessed are those who have loved ones
around them to make it happen....

DON'T CRY

Don't cry for me when I am gone

I will come back

To envelope you

As a warm blanket on a cold winter
night....

As a hot cup of coffee on a rainy day

As the first rays of the sun falling on
you....

As the first drop of rain trickling down
your face

Yes I will come back

You just need to keep looking....

UNSPOKEN WORDS

There are volumes inside me
Yearning to emerge
Words left unspoken
Feelings still unheard
I may tear open and shatter
If they stay within anymore
Give me a chance, a hope
I live everyday in anticipation
Of a tomorrow where I am heard
My words appreciated
My thoughts perceived...

BROKEN WINGS

My broken wings
Lie strewn around
As if asking me
Why did I not fly?
When the world was at my feet
Why did I wait for my prince in
Shining armour?
When I could fly alone
Soaring the heights of success
I had wings to make the world mine
But I chose to wait
For my prince to fly with me
But what I didn't know was
He didn't want me to fly
All he wanted was me to be
Tied down in chains

Never to fly again

The wings which once wanted

To take on the world

Forgot how to fly

And one day the feathers just scattered
all over

FIREFLIES

From a distance

I saw your shimmering soul

And wondered

Will this ethereal soul ever find its home
in mine?

I was bewitched by your captivating
presence

Your aura shining like a thousand
fireflies

Oh I so wished...

That you make your home in my forlorn soul

But alas!

You were looking for a light that shone
more brightly than yours

And me

I was just a soul enveloped by my own
darkness....

CONNECTION

To understand someone is to understand
their silence

Without them uttering a single word

To love someone is to love them with their
flaws

As no one is perfect and never can be

Everyone can love the external beauty

But loving the soul is what true love is
all about

The eyes are the window to the soul

They have volumes left unsaid

Seeing through them and making

a connection with the pristine soul

That is what love is.... isn't it?

FARAWAY

Sometimes I think

When I go away

Into a land unknown

Far away from the ones I love

Will anyone ever miss me?

Or will life just go on for them

The way it has always has

It worries me

To think that it's only me that loves

And no one else loves me in return

I have never been showered with affection

As far as I remember

Never have I ever been surprised

By anyone I love

It's like I am taken for granted

By everyone...

It scares me to think

That no one will miss me when I am
gone....

LIFE

The myriad hues of the sun

Brighten up our days

Blessed are we

To be a part of this miraculous life

The moon shows us the calm and serene
beauty of the night

For darkness is as important as light

We dance to the tunes of the creator

Who has created this beautiful stage?

For us to dance to our hearts delight

The rhythm and beats

Make us feel alive

Blessed are we to be the chosen ones

For this miraculous life

BROKEN

Here I am

Bruised and broken

Beyond repair

Whoever said that life is fair?

There are galaxies between us

You and me

The ranting of my shattered soul

Can you even hear?

The pieces of my soul

is a different shade of blue

There is darkness all around

The sky has a gloomy hue

The distance between us, I know

Is like a billion light years

Never can our souls ever be entwined

Ah! The yearning for your love

Can my aching heart ever recover....

RAINBOW

Everyone finds what they have been looking
for

Be it a rainbow in the sky

Or a happy moment between sad times

Be it a flicker of hope in an otherwise
despairing life

Or a ray of sunshine between the dark
clouds

Be it the warmth of a loved one on a cold
dreary day

Or a smile from a random stranger on the
street

Be it a warm hug when one is feeling low

Or a word of appreciation from that
special someone

Yes we all find what we have been looking
for

We just need to keep looking....

COMPANION

Why do we need?

A shoulder to cry on

Someone to lean on

When our soul is tired by this stressful
life

We need someone to make it better

To lift the burden from our shoulders

And put it on theirs

Even if it's for a short time

Why do we need companionship?

In this journey of life

It is to rest our tired shoulders

In someone's arms

To feel the warmth of their body

And heal our aching soul

Why do we need someone to share?

Our joys and sorrows

It's because no feeling is

complete without another soul

to share it with us...

LIFE AFTER DEATH

Where do we go from here?

Once we are through with the mundane life

What is there in store for us?

On the other side

Is there another life for us to lead?

Or is it the end

Does life go on even after death?

Or death has the final word

Does our soul come back to lead another
new life ?

Or the soul has a greater purpose

The answers to these questions evade us

Never can we ever go to the other side

And let the world know

What's in store for us when life betrays
us.....

DARLING

You light up the darkest corners of my
heart

Your soul sparks a fire in me

I am bedazzled by the sight of you

You are my pathway to eternal bliss

The moments spent with you are heavenly

It's as if I am in paradise

I am ruptured by your soothing voice

Your touch makes me ecstatic

I am in a state of euphoria when you hold
me in your arms

Oh I so wish that you light up my life
till eternity...

INSOMNIA

When I lie down to sleep

Insomnia kicks me in the face

Your memories keep clinging on to me

And my thoughts begin to race

All I look for is a haven

Where my heart gets solace

I want to run from all the terrible
memories

I long for such a place

A place my soul gets refuge

From this impenetrable mess

But alas, all that is a far-fetched
fantasy

Life is real, I cannot run away

The turmoil within me,

the insomnia hits me hard in the face...

JOURNEY

Life is not what we think it is
Life is a journey between birth
and death
Its learning to accept the
Sorrows along with the joys
Falling in love and falling out of it
Going through trials and tribulations
Winning some and losing some
Life is not an easy path
It's full of twists and turns
We never know what is in store
For us on this journey
Enjoy it till the last breath....

CHANGE

Life is all about embracing change
Letting go of the past and
accepting the new with open arms
We surely do miss the past
Be it old friends, relationships
or our old home
They stay with us forever
In the corners of our heart
But the heart should be open
and receptive to change
To newer avenues and greener pastures
That is what life is all about
Change!!

LANGUAGE OF LOVE

Do you understand the language of my
heart?

The words unsaid, the awkward silences

The fluttering of my heartbeat

Swaying to your tunes

My soul wanting to dance with yours

On the path to ecstasy

My heart gently reverberating to the sound
of your heartbeat

My eyes glancing at yours

Looking for infinite pools within

For me to drown in them

Soaking me in your love

That is what I yearn for

Learn the language of my heart

And complete the incomplete me....

LOOK WITHIN

To find yourself you need to leave behind
the voices and opinions of others who
clutter your mind

To find yourself you need to delve into
your own soul and look for the intricacies
within

To find yourself you need to forget your
past and unlearn what you have learnt from
the lesson of life

People judge you and form opinions about
you

That is not what you are

You are what you are deep within

You have a profound ocean within you

Let others not decide how they want to see
you

Be you....

PERFECTION

Is there anything as a perfect human
being?

Or do we all have our flaws

Is anyone born perfect?

Without any flaws and shortcomings?

If there is then I would want to meet that
person

I think my whole life would pass without
me coming

across a perfect human being

We all have our blemishes, our flaws

No one is perfect

We too are not

So let's not expect perfection from others

Because if we do then we will never find
satisfaction

Before looking for a perfect person

Let's try and be even close to perfection

FILTER

I wish there was a filter

So that one could decide which moments to live

And which to leave behind

Can I relive my life once again?

Those moments I wish to cherish

Which made me what I am today?

I do wish to live my life again

The same yet different

So that I can filter my life

And leave out those people who made my life a nightmare

Leave out those moments I do not wish to live again

And fully live those moments which

Made me happy and blissful

I wish there was a filter

So that I could leave out the worst

And get the best....

SAVIOUR

Ah death...The Saviour of us all
The one that takes us away
from the miseries of life
There was no more pain
All I saw was a bright white light
That engulfed me in its arms
Oh it was so alluring!!
The touch so soothing
The pain just disappeared
And all I was left with was solace
Contentment filled up my senses
All I wanted was to be there
Forever
Away from the suffering
of this world
Where we are just mere puppets
Living a life preordained

37

Decided even before our birth
Are our shares of miseries?
Ah it's lovely
The journey after death...

PHOENIX

Lift yourself up

From the worries of the world

Set yourself free from the shackles of
pain

Take off the cloak of despair

And view the world as a better place

Do not drown yourself in the sea of sorrow

Learn how to swim and fight

Against the raging storm within

Rise above the ashes like a phoenix

Don't keep smouldering from within

Burn the hopelessness and despair instead

And feel alive again....

PUPPET

As I reflect back on my life

I realise

All I have been

Is a mere puppet

First in the hands of the ones who created
me

And then in the hands of the one with whom
I was bound for life

Never have I ever been my own person, my
own self

Always dancing to their tunes

Always been steered in the direction they
want me to go

Have always been moulded according to the
shape they desire

Never have I ever

Been what I want to be....

TIME FLIES

Another year gone by

Gone in a jiffy

Seems just like a dream

A year that just whizzed past

Leaving behind mixed memories

One day our life too will be left behind

And we will exit from this drama of life

Our role will soon be over

So let's make the most of what we have
left

Before we too are just a memory...

THE GOOD AND THE BAD

Every positive thing we see
Be it a flower
Or a rainbow
Has a negative side to it
The side we do not see
Or do not want to..
Like every rose has its thorn
Only when the thorn pricks us
Do we realise that something
as beautiful as a rose too
has a negative side to it...
Same like life
We do not want to see the negativity of it
But we need to realise that in life
Good and bad walk side by side.

WORDS ARE NOT ENOUGH

Can words sum up my love for you?

Can they justify the emotions within?

The days I spent remembering you

The nights I lay wide awake

thinking about you

If in slumber then dreaming about you

The restlessness within

To touch you and

feel the warmth of your skin on mine

To hear you speak

Your words soothing my ears and
stimulating my senses

Making me reach the zenith and touching my
soul

Your eyes speaking volumes without you
uttering a single word

Can words sum up my love for you?

IS IT LOVE?

Love is such a strong word
Do we really love all the people
we say we do love?
Or is it just fondness which we
profess as love
Love is a strong emotion
One cannot love too many
It takes the crux of the
word away
It belittles the deep feeling
that love actually is
So the next time you say
you love someone
Think before you say it
Because if it's not love
Then why say it
And make a mockery out of it!!

HERE TODAY, GONE TOMORROW

Life...

We are here today

We will be gone tomorrow

We are mere travellers in this journey
called life

Travelling from the time we are born to
our death

Like actors on a stage

Enacting their role

Till their role in the play is over

We are living

Only the moments meant for us to live in

Every single breath counted

Till we breathe our last...

LOVE IS IMPERFECT

Love is all about showing your true
colours

And still being in love

Love is all about sharing your deepest
darkest secrets

And still being in love

Love is baring your soul and body

And still being in love

Love is knowing how she looks without
makeup

How she looks when she wakes up

And still being in love

Love is about loving all the imperfections

And still being in love

Love is knowing the curves of her not so
perfect body and still loving her

Love is not only about admiring the beauty

Its all about accepting the flaws

And still being in love...

BARE YOUR SOUL

Opening your heart and soul is not
something everyone is capable of

It takes a lot to open your heart and bare
your soul

It is not everyone's cup of tea

Very rarely does one come across such
remarkable people

Anyone can bare their body

But baring the soul is truly being naked

That is when you let the other person
explore the deepest corners of your body
and soul

That is what only a sensitive awakened
soul is capable of

The rest are just mere bodies entwined
with each other in a physical connect with
no spiritual connection....

LIFE AND DEATH

The distance between

The living and the dead

Can never be covered

As once dead

One can never recover

No matter how hard we try

The dead cannot come back

The body is our vehicle

Once it is destroyed

And the body is no more

The soul is what remains

The soul needs a body

So that it can connect with other human
beings

The body is the outer layer

Of the invisible soul

No matter how hard we try
The body once gone
Can never come back
The soul looks for a new body
To be whole again

LONGING

I long for you

Like the earth longs for the first rays of
the sun

To fill it up with light

I long for you

Like the barren land longs for the first
drop of rain

So that everyone can dance in delight

I long for you

Like the day longs for the dark night

So that the world can rest and sleep tight

I long for you

Like a tired traveller who longs for home

Or like weary vagabond in a desert longing
for an oasis to quench his thirst

I long for you

Like a small child longs for his mother's
warm touch

I long for you
Like a sailor longs for the sea shore
So that he can see his loved ones again
My longing I can explain
But You!! Can I ever get you back again?

GRIEF

It is said "Do not grieve"

Anything you lose comes round in another
form

Does it hold true for the one you love?

If they leave do we get them back in the
form of a new person

But are we ready to accept the new person
with open arms

Till we do not let go of the past

Of the person we loved with all our heart

Are we ready to accept a new form, a new
face?

We cannot accept the new till we do not
forget the old...

CHORDS OF MY HEART

There are lots of people that I meet

There are few who touch the chords of my
heart

Few I do not want to meet again

The ones who touch my heart

Are the ones that I want to keep in my
life forever?

But alas! Life has something else planned
for me..

The ones I want to be with do not want me
in their life

They do not feel the connect in the same
way

They do not reciprocate my feelings of
affection

I try my best to keep them in my life

What draws me to them?

And what is it about me that repel them?

The answers are a mystery

Is it me or is it them?

I wish I could know....

LOVE IS LIFE

Love is not just a four letter word

It means the 'world'

Love is the reason why the world goes
around

Without love the world would have ceased
to exist

Love is about capturing someone's heart
and soul..

But only if the other person's heart is
roused in the same way

Love can never be forced

Feelings can never be coerced

If it is then it isn't love

Love is all about giving and forgiving

Love is about holding on yet learning to
let go

To love is to be in a state of euphoria
yet the heart beats like it's in dysphoria

Strange are the feelings of love

The heart and mind are always at conflict
Always denying the existence of the other
But in the end if you get the one you love
The battle is won
But if you lose then your agony has just
begun....

LESSONS OF LIFE

Life teaches us a lot of lessons

Some we want to learn

The bitter ones we do not want to learn

But sadly it does not give us any choices

As life is a combination of the good and
bad

The ugly and the beautiful

Sadness and happiness is a part and parcel
of the game of life

No matter what life throws at us

We should always be positive

And lift ourselves up even in despair

Do not give life a chance to put you down

Instead lift yourself up and show life
what you are made of...

PAIN

Somewhere someone is trying to switch
their heart off from all the pain...

But in this big bad world

Pain is the only thing you gain

If you are selfless everyone looks at you
with disdain

So before facing this world switch off
your conscience

Because if you don't then you lose
everything

And all goes in vain....

INTROSPECTION

Nights are often the time

When I sit back and introspect

About where I went wrong in life

What made me make those choices that I did

Was it an ordinary human wanting the best
out of life?

Or my soul looking for true love and
happiness

But time and again

My choices were proven incorrect

My decisions flawed

Where did I go wrong?

In trying to find love

In trying to find life....

MIRACLE

Life is a miracle

Yet so unreliable and unpredictable

We are here now living this moment

But no one is invincible

We plan for our future

For the time which is unseen

But life has its own ways of crashing in
between

We say we will love forever

But forever who has seen?

So lets take a vow

And live in the present

That is "Now"....

HEAL ME

I put on a brave face for the world to see

But deep inside the silence is just
killing me

The words left unsaid, the emotions
unexpressed are pleading to thee

Heal me please heal me...

SOLITUDE

When the world abandons me
Solitude lends me a hand
When the world leaves me alone
Solitude is my companion
I am captivated by my solitary self
Because it does not desert me when
everyone else does..

WHY TO JUDGE ?

We all are judged..

By the way we write

If we write about heartbreak

The world thinks we have been through it

If we write about love

People think we are in love

If we write about unrequited love

Then maybe we have gone through it

Strange isn't it....

Yes no doubt we all go through a myriad of
emotions and experiences in our lifetime

We all break and get back up on our feet
again

Writers can feel all those emotions even
if they haven't experienced them

So never judge a writer....

BROKEN BUT BEAUTIFUL

Next time someone calls you broken..

Tell them...Yes I am broken but still
beautiful!!

Your beauty is not what others see

But its deep down inside your heart..

It's your ability to love unconditionally.

Next time someone calls you broken

Tell them...Yes I am broken but still
beautiful!!

MYSTERY

People do not understand

The mystery that I am

They are scared to unravel the deepest
corners of my heart

They are petrified to unfurl the layers of
my tangled soul

They get intimidated by the illusion that
is my mind

They feel they have to break open the
facade that I show to the world

So they detach themselves from my being

That is why I am left alone...alone in
this chaotic world

DARKNESS

I love the darkness of the night
The time I drift off to sleep
For in my dreams we are together
No one can take me away from you
That is my solace
But when I wake up and you are not there
My heart is torn into pieces
Yes I love the darkness of the night
That is when we are together...

SOULMATE

There is a voice which wants to be heard
A soul which wants to be touched
A heart which wants to beat like no other
It longs for a soul mate
A soul which hears its silence
A heart that beats like its own....

MEMORY LANE

Sometimes I go on a trip down memory lane

Thinking about what was and what could
have been

What I did and what I could have done
differently

My mistakes and the tribulations that
followed

Were they meant to be?

Was that my destiny?

I wish I knew the answers

Of what was and what could have been

Sometimes I wish I could change

a few things back then

Would my life be any different?

From what it is now?

I wish I knew the answers

I so wish I could rewrite my destiny.....

ETERNAL LOVE

How beautiful would it be to find someone
who is in love with your soul

Your inner beauty is what they desire

The external body is just a layer

But the soul is what is truly beautiful

How lovely will it be

To be loved for the wonderful soul that
you possess

Someone who truly wants you for what you
are deep within

Someone who understands the intricacies of
your soul

And loves you for who you are

External beauty fades with time

But the soul remains immortal

DEEP IN MY HEART

Of all the things that I possess

My favourite is my memory of you

You are my prized possession

Never to leave the confines of my heart

Though you no longer belong to me

But the memories remain

Like trophies on the shelf deep inside me

You are something that will always be

Etched on the walls of my heart

EPITOME OF STRENGTH

A woman has the strength to change the
world

Make it a better place

The world goes on because it is she who
gives birth to life

She is a homemaker as well as a career
woman

She knows how to maintain the perfect
balance

She has the power to multitask

Her heart is brimming with the love she
has to give

You can see the world in her eyes as they
are deep as oceans

A woman is incomparable

So why just one day as Women's day

Let everyday be a celebration as she makes
the world go round

DESIRE TO BE LOVED

Why do we need love

Love is there everywhere

Even within us

Why do we need someone to complete us

When we ourselves are complete

A flower blooms

Giving fragrance to all

Without expecting anything in return

Why do we humans expect love

If we give our love to someone

Why are we looking for love outside

When it's within us.

THE GIRL NO ONE NOTICED

Yes she was there

Standing in a corner

Her eyes brimming with tears

Hiding them from the world

She was the girl no one noticed

Her silence speaking volumes

If someone cared to notice

Solitary in her grief

Her eyes carrying stories untold

About the pain and angst she had been
through

She loved with all her heart

But yet went unnoticed

Forgotten by the world

She was the girl no one noticed

But she had the world inside her....

GOD

If I were God

I would have created life differently

Life would not have been so fragile

Living would not have been this futile

Because thats how it is now

We are alive but we do not know for how
long will we breathe

Life is unreliable as the next moment is
unpredictable

Will we get to see the next moment, the
next day?

Our life is controlled by our breath

The day we stop breathing everything is
terminated

If I were God

I would have created life differently

SUFFOCATION

Suffocated to the core

It's like she cannot breathe

This life does not let her live the way
she desires

She is choking, her throat dry and parched

Her heart pounding inside her

Ready to burst out any moment

Asking her to get out of this mess

Before it kills her

Why let your dreams and desires be caged
inside of you

One life we get isn't it?

What is life if we cannot live it the way
we desire

Why does the world want to control us in
whatever we do

The desires want a way out

But the world does not let us live....

STORM

The storm

It came suddenly out of nowhere

Without any warning

And ripped me apart

And I stood there thinking

How could someone have the power to rip me
apart

And shatter me

But yes you did that to me

When you left suddenly without warning

I was shattered

It felt like a storm was ripping me apart

I had nothing to hold on to

Nothing after it left.....

WINTER

It's cold and dreary outside
Just like the inside of my heart
Winter refuses to leave
Like you refuse to leave my thoughts
I so want summer back in my life
Am tired of this winter
It's gnawing at my soul
Leaving me empty
Just like a void refusing to be filled
My mind is filled up with memories of what
was
I want happiness to embrace me once again
Will the winter ever leave my heart
Will I be able to move on...
Will summer come once again?

RESTLESS

My soul craves for you

My body hungers for you

My heart beats for you

My eyes moist with the memories of what
was

And what could have been

We could have been magic together

But magic you did not believe in

The evenings bring

A strange kind of restlessness along

I wish you were here

I wish we could sing a beautiful song

A song full of love

A place where we belong

But it's just me who saw the beauty of our
love

Just me who thought it wasn't wrong

Now it's me and your memory

Restlessness is now with me lifelong....

NO ONE

No one will come to wipe away your tears

No one is going to treat you the way you
want to be treated

No one is going to love you the way you
want

No one will understand you the way you
want to be understood

No one will ever understand your silence,
the language of your heart

So love yourself, understand yourself

Live for yourself

Alone we are and will always be

Be your own best friend.....

LONG GONE

You are long gone

From my life

But my heart refuses to give up on you

It still longs for you

Like the world longs for the first rays of
the sun

The earth longs for the first drop of rain

I know you are long gone

And are not coming back

But the heart still hopes

For you....

LOOK FOR LOVE

Look for love

In the smallest of things

A bird chirping

A pet licking your face

A warm hug by a friend

A beautiful sunrise

The first drop of rain

A beautiful rainbow

The wind blowing on your face

Flowers blooming

If this isn't love...

What is??

JUST LIKE THAT

Sometimes I can't even write a line

No matter how hard I try

But sometimes words just flow

It's as if there are volumes inside me

Waiting to be written

The yearning, the heartbreak, the
bitterness

All come out word by word

To form a heartbreaking poem

It's as if a sculpture is getting carved

To make a beautiful piece of art....

HEARTBREAK

Has your heart been broken?

By someone you love

As you do not know how to love anymore

You are carrying the weight of the broken
heart with you

Wherever you go

No matter who falls for you

And tries to make you fall in love.. yet
again

You never stop carrying the baggage of the
past

It's as if there is a big weight on your
shoulders

And in your heart

That can never make you fall in love again

Till you try and lift it up from your
shoulders and your heart

And then you will be able to love...once
again

SOLACE

Deep within
The soul remains untouched
Looking for solace
The thirst never quenched
The body devoured
All desires unfolding onto the body
As if the body is what one seeks
But the soul
Never understood
It remains a mystery
Me, Yes me!!
I am more than a body
I am a soul
With unrelinquished desires
Deep within me
Fill up my senses
Make my soul complete
Let me be whole....

AMISS

There is something amiss between
you and me
A lacuna which cannot be filled
An empty space which can
never be occupied
No matter how hard we try
To build a bridge between us
Or to mend the gap
The space cannot be filled up
As it never was
And never will be your wish....

SONG OF LIFE

The lyrics of the song of life
Are composed by the creator
We just have to sing along to his music
And dance to his tunes
Sometimes the music is jarring
Sometimes soothing
We just need to keep pace with the rhythm
And sing along

DEW DROPS

You were like the first rain of the
monsoon

Tingling my senses

Wiping away all the

Unwholesomeness of my tired soul

The first dew drops of a wet cold morning

Falling on me

Making me come alive

With your purity

You were like the first rays of the
morning sun

Waking me up from my deep slumber

Cleansing me from within

I now am just a tired soul

Longing for you

To make me whole again....

LIFE IS A GAME

Isn't it a mockery

This Life

We are mere players in this game

Some win some lose

Some play their part better than the
others

But our destiny is not in our hands

It is written for us way before we are
born

We can only live it

It's like our destiny is mocking at us

And telling us that we can never win

In this fight against it

Life is already the winner

And we are the losers

PASSION

The sky turned a little stormy

When she looked at it with passion

Her deep blue eyes speaking volumes

Making the sky wild and untamed

The rain started to fall on her face

Drenching her curly locks

Wetting her sensuous lips as if trying to
kiss her

She smiled and the sky got wilder and
fierce

Just like an untamed animal

Who wanted to satiate it's hunger

The more she smiled the wilder it got...

HOPE

Hope is the thing we fear

Yes it is

We fear what we hope for

What if our hopes and dreams are not
fulfilled

What if we do not get what we hope for?

What if our dreams are shattered and our
faith is broken

What if?

Yes, hope is the thing we fear....

UNREVEALED FACT

Can we hold ourselves responsible?

For the decisions we take in life

No matter how good or how flawed they are

Or is it that our decisions are not our
decisions

But they are chosen for us

Can we be blamed for whatever we do wrong?

Or has it been pre-decided by the one who
creates us

The master of the universe

The creator of our destiny....

LANGUAGE OF MY HEART

Do you understand the language of my heart?

The words unsaid, the awkward silences

The fluttering of my heartbeat

Swaying to your tunes

My soul wanting to dance with yours

On the path to ecstasy

My heart gently reverberating to the sound of
your heartbeat

My eyes glancing at yours

Looking for infinite pools within

For me to drown in them

Soaking me in your love

That is what I yearn for

Learn the language of my heart

And complete the incomplete me....

SILENT LOVE

I could feel your love
Though we were miles apart
In the words left unsaid
In the silence between us
That spoke volumes
Without us saying a single word...

UNHEARD

What does it mean to be a woman?

It means that you are seen but not heard

You can speak but no one listens

Your voice goes unheard

You don't live but you just exist

You are shunned by the so called stronger sex

You give up your entire life for others but
you do not get credit for the same

You bring a new life into this world

The world exists because of you

But your contribution is never acknowledged

You go through so much pain

Only to be looked down upon

You are tortured and humiliated because you
are a woman

A woman never gets her due....

STRINGS

I look for strings

The ones that tie me to you

I see no strings

All I see are chains

My soul hurts

Suffocated and choked

I long to be set free

Setting each other free is what a
relationship should be

Not bondage....

IN SEARCH OF PEACE

The roads are clogged

I am on my way home

People everywhere

Suffocating me from within

I cannot breathe

The dust is inside my nostrils

Its killing me slowly

This chaotic world

Its a mess..this world

Let me reach home

So that I may rest in peace....

MYSTERY OF LIFE

Are the ones who express better human beings?

Because they tell one and all about how they
feel

What is inside them is not a mystery

They are an open book which everyone can read

On the other hand the ones who are quiet are a
closed book which no one has read

They are a mystery which has not been unfolded

They are misunderstood

But does that make them inferior human beings?

I look for answers within me...

Because I am one of them

Am I? Am I not?

Or should I let you all decide...

WHEN YOU WERE THERE

With you around me I felt as if I was home

My heart had made your heart its home

I had no worries in the world

It was a beautiful abode

Full of dreams and fantasies

I could be myself

I felt on top of the world

It was the best place to be in

I was home

But sometimes some homes are not meant for us
to stay in forever

Especially someone's heart

It can never be a permanent abode

I was bereft of love and happiness

I was homeless....

LIFE GOES ON

Before I was born

Little did I know?

That life is a cycle

What has come must go one day

The old giving way to the new

Childhood moving towards Youth

Youth towards Middle age

And then Old age

Which is the last lap in the race of life?

And eventually the cycle of life gets over

To be born again

Reborn at another place and time

And start the cycle of life again.....

LOVE YOURSELF

Revolving your life around one person is
wrong

Because when they leave

Your world stops

As they were the only person

making your world goes round

Love yourself instead

Make yourself the centre of your universe

Because you will be the only one who will
never leave....

MIRAGE

You ask me if I am afraid of dying

Yes I am

Because I haven't lived yet

I may be living

But I am not alive

I want to live a life where I am

loved and understood

Live a life with someone who makes me come
alive

Someone who is full of life

Who makes me laugh

Just with a twinkle in their eyes

Someone who understands my silence

And appreciates my words

You ask me if I am afraid of dying

Yes, it's because I haven't lived yet....

SHACKLES

Am I a bird in a cage

Suffocated and bound by the shackles of
society

Or am I a free bird

Flying high in the deep blue sky

I am a woman

A woman can fly high if her wings are not
severed

She has her dreams and aspirations

She can achieve her goals if she is given
an opportunity

But alas..she is no more than a bird in
captivity...

FIGMENT OF MY IMAGINATION

I kept looking for you
In the different chapters of my life
Life kept passing me by
But never did I find you
You only existed
In my thoughts
You were nothing but
a figment of my imagination....

www.ingramcontent.com/pod-product-compliance
Lightning Source LLC
LaVergne TN
LVHW010239200726
843506LV00014B/3054